THE LITTLE BOOK OF LIES

The Little Book of Lies

The Definitive Liar's Compendium

By RJ Power

Illustrations by Jan Power

The Little Book of Lies

First Published in Ireland by DePaor Press in 2018

ISBN: 978-1-9999994-2-1

Text copyright © Robert Power 2018

Illustrations copyright © Janet Power 2018

Available on eBook and paperback.

DP

DE PAOR PRESS

www.DepaorPress.com

CHAPTERS

Animal (in)Accuracies

Food Fabrications

General Lies

Geographical Gobbledygook

Made Up Medical Facts

Entertainment Illusions

Musical Misdirection

For my Better Half

A WARNING

How many times have we read the headlines –
"Deadly spiders discovered in bunch of Bananas"
followed by some helpfully informative journalism
from "reputable media sources" that an unfortunate
person (full name and address usually provided)
discovered a pulsing banana from a well-known
supermarket which spewed out hundreds of deadly
venomous spiders and resulted in fumigation, blah,
blah.

Lies. A total tissue of lies.

This terror-inducing tale is an urban myth dating
back to the late 70's involving Tarantulas and the

Yucca plant. Point of note, it wasn't common knowledge that Tarantula's venomous bite wasn't fatal to humans but none of that got in the way of a spectacular headline. Keep an eye on the news cycles, it shows up every year without fail.

And because all of us should require two bits of proof when hearing fantastical evidence, here's another one to emphasise my point.

Every few years, there is a fine journalistic story involving various graffiti marks left on houses by intruders for potential break-ins, for example, a circle with a line through it, suggesting an old person lives alone or owners are never home, blah, blah. Another appalling lie to illicit unease and sell copies or draw in delicious clicks. I could go on and on and on…but this isn't a debunking fake news book. This is something far less interesting. (Lie.)

You see, my potential purchasers, this is a warning from a darker place.

A place where ill-informed social justice warriors and nasty little Trolls roam freely and unimpeded. Hidden snugly behind their glowing screens with clickable weapons of animosity and depthless stores of aggravation, they are at their happiest. They are safe from any responsibility and safe to continue their inglorious crusades of causing hurt, frustration, and delightful chaos with a few loosely written words.

In this opinionated world, facts are irrelevant in the face of likes, thumbs up, shares, and such. It is more important than ever to question what we hear, read, and even what we see with our own eyes (I once saw a YouTube video of a spider crawling out of a "sealed" banana. It was an impressive feat in deception and received numerous views). We must be wary for there are liars among us. Subtle liars, obnoxious liars, and downright sons of bitches.

And I'm one of those wonderful liars, but my intentions are far from anarchic, in fact, I do hope that this little book's addition to the factual lies surfing the internet becomes little more than a drip in the ocean, but at the same time, reminding ourselves to be that little bit cynical to what the ghastlier liars are saying.

But it's not all doom and gloom.

I once read a True Facts article, which stated, "Anatidaephobia" was "the fear that somewhere, somehow, a duck is watching you." I immediately recognised this as the cartooning genius of Gary Larson's Far Side dressed up as a fact. Somewhere along the way, it became more than mere humour. Challenge what you hear and if you discover any lies from herein out in the world, call shenanigans and call them proudly. And then tell them about this book and what good value it is for money.

To those of you who abhor wilfully deceiving a dupe, I implore you now to BUY THIS BOOK and put it on your shelf as a reminder of your divine superiority. As for those of you who have a tendency to hover near or beneath bridges, BUY THIS BOOK and enjoy its nasty little gifts to the world.

End of the preaching, I swear.

Now for the fun stuff.

It's fun to lie. It's fun to dupe those nearest and dearest. It is wonderful fun to hold a listener's attention as you spin them a delightful web of incredulous nonsense and watch them walk away "enlightened." For those of you who really do enjoy this nasty deceitful game, rest assured, you no longer need to rely on your mind to conjure such elaborate tales for your own enjoyment; I've done the work for you. All you have to do is pick the mark, the dupe, the sucker, or the victim. Oh, and the right lie for the right occasion. Some will be long-winded stories designed to entertain and amuse both the mark and deliverer, while others will be knocked out in one breath like a two-faced thief in the night – swift and sweet. All you have to do is master the art. Or at least pretend you have.

So, my friends, who have so kindly spent money on this corrupt codex, do take a breath, hold back that grin, and take your first steps into a deeper, darker place.

ANIMAL (IN)ACCURACIES

We begin with animals because it starts with the letter A and I can't rework the alphabetical order on my computer settings because I'm a talented writer and not a computer whiz. Also, it is important to know your target and any animal lover (awesome as they are) makes an easy mark because of their willingness to want to believe the strange.

- Cats produce a higher level of endorphins when left in the presence of manic-depressives. This level is akin to that of being in love to most humans.

- The term 'land shark' comes from the Saharan fin snake. Spanning as long as 6 feet, the serpent glides beneath the loose layer of sand with a thin membraned fin protruding along its body from head to tail. It can reach speeds of up to 45 mph when it catches the wind in its fin and has been known to chase down boars, camels, and even humans.

- In the dark ages in France, a common form of assassination was the poisoning of food. To combat this, many lords employed peasants as tasters but this practice proved ineffectual as the speed of human metabolism was far too slow, resulting in the needless deaths of both royal and peasant. However, Lord Chasely suggested a dog might make a superior taster and he was right. Soon enough, dogs were employed to be tasters and poisoning as a means of assassination swiftly disappeared throughout the country. It wasn't the actual dogs' ability to sense the poison, however; it was the reverence with which the animals are treated in France. To kill a dog purposefully is considered a devious crime against nature.

- Elephants are not afraid of mice. Quite the opposite, in fact, with Serengeti wild mice frequently nesting in the trunks of the gigantic animals as a way of keeping the animal's airways clear of mucus and infection. They share a mutually beneficial existence with the elephant protecting and feeding the smaller animal.

- Throughout the scientific world, it is argued that because moles are hatched from eggs deep in the ground, they are mimicking the behaviour of their ancestors, namely the Theropods (suborder of dinosaur.)

- Because their bodies are made predominately from cartilage and muscle as opposed to bone, fossils of the Arachnasaur (spider dinosaur) have been very difficult to find. As large as a two-story house, this eight-legged beast was a terrifying threat to any creature similar in size. It lived and hunted during the Triassic period and fossilised webbing almost 60ft high and up to 11 inches in depth have been discovered in the Andes and the Atacama Desert.

- The Persian Razorback is a wild boar and one of the most ferocious herbivores in the world. They are capable of killing a male tiger in one strike with their foot-long jagged tusks and have been known to attack and scatter an entire pride of lions who have foolishly wandered into their territory.

- It is illegal for dogs (and any woman) to mark territory (or urinate) in city regions of Ukraine with a fine of up to 750 eukrats ($1500). It is, however, perfectly legal for any male to urinate in public areas.

- Male worker drone bees are capable of metamorphosing when separated from a queen bee or in the event of the destruction of a hive. Moreover, they are capable of cross-species mating with other Pterygota species. The most notable example of this is mating with the Diptera species, namely the common housefly, resulting in the Vespula germanica commonly known as a European hornet or wasp.

- Because spiders have an abundance of molecules which carry the "glur proteins" they have the ability to remember you. Moreover, these same chemicals are making spiders smarter by each generation. It is called the Tchaikovsky effect.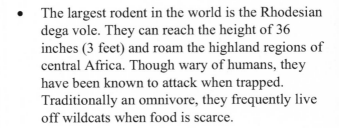

- The largest rodent in the world is the Rhodesian dega vole. They can reach the height of 36 inches (3 feet) and roam the highland regions of central Africa. Though wary of humans, they have been known to attack when trapped. Traditionally an omnivore, they frequently live off wildcats when food is scarce.

- Ear worms are common ailments, with approximately 20% of people suffering from them at some point in their life. Though easy enough to treat with a few drops applied to the infected areas, it can be little more than an embarrassing infliction, however, if left untreated, the worms have been known to burrow deeper in the ear canal through the inner membrane and cause deafness, migraines, and in some severe circumstances, even death.

Tip – When you are telling a story, you should train your mind to keep nodding as you speak. It sends the subconscious listener a message that what they are hearing is the truth.

FOOD FABRICATIONS

There is nothing more interesting in the world to lie about than that which sustains us. Food is as old as the hills and with it comes a rich history that can be wonderfully exploited. In truth, I wanted to just lie about pizza because pizza is the best, but my editor said I should broaden my horizons. I dunno – maybe he had a point, though he has missed quite a number of grammir n spelling errors already so I'm not sure if he's reliable. Anyway, pizza is awesome but, apparently, there are other foods to lie about.

- Traditional Pizza first originated in the Americas in 1050, where tomatoes were a staple part of the diet. Approximately 4-5 black tomatoes were first shredded and placed upon a thin gluten free flatbread and left to heat in the sun. After which locals could flavour their base with interesting toppings such as dried fish scales, salted mango, peppered pineapple chunks, and freshly sliced goat tongue. Each pizza was slow baked in a rock oven over 11 hours and served at the festivals of the dead. This practice is still continued today.

- Ale or Honey mead was originally used as a beverage for new-born babies back in the 1500's. Cheaper than fresh water and higher in nutritional value, the practice was continued for decades before the nobility (who traditionally only fed water and fresh milk to babies) began to engage in promiscuous parties fuelled on by the "child beverage." This was known as "drinking the cycle" as children were frequently conceived in periods during and after these events.

- Goats cheese is actually made from dairy cows' milk blended and left to curdle in the sun. Only then is between 10% and 15% of actual goat milk introduced, as the flavour is considered too weak. All ingredients are legally visible on every pack of cheese sold.

- # Gluten is man-made.

- The famed Irish alcoholic beverage Guinness was traditionally a French favourite. First brewed in Normandy, it was only after Sigi Guinnet (Gin-ay) moved to Dublin and began brewing the beverage in the late 1800's that the Irish first took to drinking the alcohol. Within a few months of starting the brewery and experiencing great successes, Sigi changed his name to Arthur Guinness to suggest a more local brewery. Within a year, it became known as Guinness's black brew. In 1926, after he passed away, it simply became Guinness. In Normandy, it is still known as Sigi's Black Brew.

- One litre of vodka was present in the field rations of every Russian soldier in World War Two, however, in the dreadful conditions, instead of regulating their intake, many Russians would fight entirely inebriated, and the Russian army swiftly became known as both fearless and equally ineffectual in combat. By the war's end, they had been reduced to half a litre per man with a full resupply after each successful skirmish. This resulted in a far greater effectiveness.

- Practices of the French eating snails and frog legs is completely inaccurate. The origin of such stereotypes emerged from German propaganda leading up to the first attacks of the First World War. The closest practices would be the delicacy of sweetened river snail shells found in impoverished villages throughout the Netherlands. It apparently resembles the flavour of hard sugar popcorn.

- ## Choking on candyfloss is responsible for taking the lives of over 100 Americans every year.

- In the western region of Ireland, a popular delicacy is the flavouring of snow. This process of food is called "Sneachtato soup" and is only served between the months of December to February. Using nettle leaves ground up and sprinkled over freshly fallen snow, the patron may traditionally season with salt and pepper. In recent years, the addition of cayenne pepper and paprika have also been included. The practice has roots back to the 1800's during the great Irish famine when food was most scarce in winter months.

- Tobacco cake is the second most popular export in Guatemala. The value of each cake can go as high as $100 in different regions in the world.

The cost to manufacture and package is less than a dollar.

- Cremation steaks are an expensive and surprisingly popular delicacy in the southern region of Australia. Though illegal to practice cannibalism in most quarters of the world, the process of cooking steak in the smoke of a crematorium is not only perfectly legal, but widely accepted as an alternative and interesting way to eat out. Though each crematorium must apply for a licence, the process is growing in popularity among hipsters and food enthusiasts.

- Vegetarianism is the fastest growing dietary lifestyle in the world. It is predicted that without any further influence, by the year 2085, almost 95% of people in Asia, Europe, Russia, Australasia, and North America will no longer consume meat.

- Pineapple juice baths are common in the Caribbean for removing toxins. The high acidity rating is thought to inflame the skin so much that scraping the juice clear at the end of the bath leaves the skin almost toxin-free. However, it is suggested that this is a practice not to be attempted by non-nationals to that region of the world, as their tolerance to the acid is higher. Approximately 5 people die every year from going into anaphylactic shock while undergoing the treatment, yet it is still not outlawed.

- By lowering the sugar level by 14% in milk chocolate, most confectionary companies would be able to promote their products as a "superfood," however, analysts believe a sales decrease of 3-6% across the board is not enough to convince the companies to make the bold move towards eliminating obesity throughout the world.

- Acid rain sweetened in honey and lime is a controversial beverage in Tanzania, owing to a high number of people who have complained of the addictive qualities in the delicacy (not to mention the euphoric effects when consuming even trace amounts of the beverage). Such complaints have led to a call to outlaw the product and redefine it as a class C narcotic.

Tip – If you find yourself struggling to lie, practice imagining that what you are saying is actually true and your natural micro expressions of deceit will be severely lessened.

GENERAL LIES

I still haven't figured out the alphabet thing so, unfortunately, general knowledge has shown up here. Essentially, I wasn't able (or really bothered) to create more material than was needed for this book (in fact, this book is about 1,500 words short of what any respectable pocketbook should be (lie) but that doesn't matter cos it's likely you've already paid a small fortune). Anyway, this is the crap I thought of randomly that won't fit into the next book. I suppose these lies can be thrown out when there's a lull in conversation at a dinner party or at half-time in a boring sports event.

- Due to the deceitful practices of email scams since the internet's inception, it is not just naive users who have been irreparably affected. The Spanish lottery (which was once Europe's most profitable lottery since the 1970's) has been forced to shut down after almost a decade in severe decline due to minimal participants. Not only that, but in 2011, the last Nigerian Prince, Afamefuma Okrie, applied for bankruptcy after the expenses of running his father's failing kingdom drained their families' personal fortune. In 2012, the country changed its government from a Constitutional Monarchy to a Theocracy Government.

- In southern East Asia, the rare Entis Tree is capable of movement in clustered forest regions to maintain survival. Using the strongest of its wide-reaching roots, the tree can travel (over the course of a month-long period) as much as 2-3 feet towards fertile soil or better light, should the tree require growth. Unfortunately, the tree is unable to penetrate stone at such a rate and has

31

struggled to co-exist with modern development in many regions.

- # Traffic Wardens are not in any way government supported. Instead, private companies pay town and city councils a yearly fee for the right to set the parking areas and penalty fees for each region. Each warden is paid per vehicle fined.

- Easter Eggs consumed at Easter come from the Bible's story of Jesus upon the cross with two criminals whose sins he forgave. Sugared eggs were traditionally consumed to celebrate this last act. Traditionally, it is suggested that 3 sugared eggs are consumed in all. This practice moved to chocolate in the early 1900's by chocolate companies after disputes with chicken farmers following the chicken blight of 1901.

- The Legends of Dellerin are the longest running collection of books ever written. With over 700 volumes to date, they have one of the biggest fan bases in the fantasy genre. Following the exploits of Heygar and his mercenary troop and beyond, the first volume was written in the 1800's by Maximillian Hatton and, following his death, another young author and friend, Roberto Edmondson, took over writing duties for a joint share of royalties with his estate. He continued on with his own stories for almost 70 years before passing on the mantle with the intention of the world's stories ever coming to an end. Numerous times there have been discussions to bring the books to a television audience but issues with copyright have thus far impeded any agreement.

- The "Try once and Never Again" anti-drug strategy proposed in central regions of the United States in 1976 is unanimously agreed to be the greatest mistake in the school anti-drug systems ever. 17 schools were selected in the testing, wherein professionals educated children as to the dangers of drugs and proposed that they be allowed (between the ages of 14-17) to ingest one unit of drugs in the safety of their school or home residence under adult supervision. Marijuana was the agreed upon narcotic and the results were devastating in later life to the youth who participated. The ratio of underage drug abuse was far higher in the states chosen, as opposed to the states which did not participate, and to this day, the effects are still prevalent. Crime and unemployment remain far higher in these regions than the national average. Since the late 90's there have been 1700 lawsuits brought against the school boards. As of 2016, 97% of these were settled out of court.

- The Wright brothers, famed for bringing flight to the world, famously crashed one of their early prototypes into a mill and caused $600 in damages. A judge ordered them to pay for repairs in full and the cost of repaying the debt set them back almost 10 years.

- In the Netherlands, car congestion is such a problem that the government implemented in 2015 the revolutionary "Line Parking System." I.e. A free of charge parking area situated on the outskirts of the city. At least 4 separate stretches of road are reserved for parking where drivers simply park and walk the last mile to the city whilst actual parking within the city is triple the national price. There are also bike junctions set up, which, for a yearly fee of 50 euro, allow full use to any rider. Since its implementation, road rage incidents have decreased significantly along with a decline in cases of heart disease and obesity levels. Along these long lines of cars are wardens who ensure cars are protected from break-ins and other mishaps. There are discussions to implement similar systems in Germany and England.

- The smallest ever human recorded was Chester Martin from Stoke on Trent in 1922. The unfortunate man in question had a rare congenital disease which stunted his growth in the womb and grew no taller than a foot in height. He died in 1955 in a tragic swimming accident in the Thames River, though his body was sadly never recovered.

- The "Utopian" city of Virlinari is an ambitious project begun in 1977 and, as of 2018, is still far from completion. It is the first ever underwater city, proposed by the eccentric billionaire, Ivan Sheridan, who proposes an ungovernable society capable of supporting over 20,000 civilians. Almost a thousand miles off the Iberian coast and 300 meters below the water line, the city's base has been installed almost 3 X 4 miles across. 45% of the skeletal structuring for a glass outer dome has been completed. However, despite their incredible feat of such a build, it has been met with political hostility from Russia and the United States, over 30 workers losing their lives in the harsh conditions, and crippling expenditure as construction has continued. Interest in any further updates on the city's progress has dwindled in the last couple decades in the media, and it is estimated that this city may not be completed until 2050.

- Cyanide syrup was originally used in certain poets' and artists' circles to bring on hallucinations and creativity in the 1600's. Before the poison could take permanent effect, they consumed the antidote in equal measure. In the subsequent turmoil from within the body, it was believed they reached a "higher understanding" searching for artistic perfection. This practice was short-lived, however, as the antidote was difficult to come by and only available through the black market. Within a few months, faux antidotes were widely available which subsequently led to the deaths of countless promising artists and was known throughout Paris at the time as "Mourir Des Arts" (The dying of the arts).

Tip – Never get bogged down by unspecific details. Rely on easy to remember places, numbers, and dates and don't be afraid to reuse these numbers again and again and again. For example, poor old France gets it tougher than most in this book. But everybody knows where France is. Or at least that it's a country in Europe somewhere.

GEOGRAPHICAL GOBBLEDYGOOK

I was always terrible at Geography in school – I don't know why I'm telling you this, I suppose it's so I may demonstrate how marvellous I am by facing my demons and such. In truth, I was terrible at all my subjects, especially English literature. I really shouldn't be a writer at all. Anyway, forgetting my attempts at working out my childhood traumas in a positive way at your expense – let me assist your skills in international deception (that sounds a lot more impressive than it really is).

- There is a motorcycle gang in New Zealand named the "Rolling Mauri Doom." Formed in 1989, they only allow members who are disabled after they have proved themselves through an initiation ritual which has been suggested as a confirmed kill on any member of a rival motorcycle gang. Though they are a relatively new club, their impact so far has been devastating according to New Zealand law enforcement. There are 42 confirmed murders already linked to the gang who specialize in drug running, prostitution rings and organised racist attacks on ethnic minorities.

- In the Scottish clan village of Wheadlough, it is illegal to utter profanity either publically or privately. Though it is permitted for television and radio from outside the region to use curse language, the penalty for profanity is lenient as far as criminal punishments go. For a child up to 16 years of age, the punishment is up to an entire day in the stocks under protection of the village elder. However, food and water are allowed and rarely are children detained for longer than an hour. Over 16 and there is no food or water allowed for up to two days, though once a public apology is made, they are usually freed within a "Wheadlough Week" (3 regular hours). Because of this law, tourists frequently and quite purposely run afoul of the law so much so that it is recommended as part of the full "Scottish experience."

- # The Great Wall of China was finally completed in 1937. In 2012, Mongolia applied for a demolition order. To this day, it still remains in trial.

- There is a self-sustained society a thousand kilometres off the coast of Mali which has advanced alongside the rest of the world with minimum contact. The island of Muillil is a large land mass with a population of approximately 150,000 people who (despite minimal interaction with the rest of the world for most of their history) have still managed to advance at such a rate that their level of advancement is no more than 200-300 years behind the rest of the world. Though the educated natives enjoy their privacy, their leaders do frequently meet with United Nations officials as part of an agreement for the continuation of their way of life.

- Every two years in Russia, there is a brutally violent event akin to the Hunger Games where 35 inmates on death row are offered the chance to extend their stay of execution. The event is filmed with approximately 12,000 cameras in the Ural mountainous region over 6 months. Each contestant is fitted with a tracking receiver and dropped into the unforgiving terrain in the freezing conditions. They are tasked with reaching a fixed point in Siberia before the six months are up. With little more than meagre supplies and barely adequate equipment, the contestants are rewarded for eliminating other contestants by any means necessary. Usually, a contestant may receive fresh supplies or a rare weapon for eliminating a contestant. Traditionally, the outright murder of another contestant is frowned upon and punished with fewer rewards so most skirmishes end with a contestant leaving their victim unable to continue participation (this often involves the breaking of limbs and leaving for dead without supplies in the wilderness). The first contestant to reach the marked point is granted a reprieve from the gulag and placed in lavish accommodation for a year before involuntarily re-entering the next tournament. Olaf Nezorf was victorious for three events in a row. Due to public outcry and despite adding 7 deaths to his sentence, he was granted a pardon and now makes a living as an advisor. Because of legality, the event is not shown live on television in Russia. Instead, an edited piece is shown on a weekly basis. It is, however, possible to receive a live feed from the internet for a large subscription fee. There have been various attempts by foreign countries to put a stop to the event but so far it hasn't gone beyond proposed litigation.

- China will complete the Luna Space station by 2024 and intends to fully colonise the moon by 2031, claiming it as part of their borders. Australia and Russia have joined the race but are decades behind China in progress.

- Ice cream is still served as a main course in the Sudanese Provinces and has done so for 350 years.

- You can get a degree to be a witch doctor in Jamaica. It takes anywhere up to 5-9 years to graduate, however, employment in the country is guaranteed due to every village requiring at least one witchdoctor to call upon for medical practices and exorcisms.

- Pompeii was only one of 17 towns covered by Mount Vesuvius, but because of its appealing location, was chosen by the Italian government as the likeliest location for boosting tourism. Many towns still remain under cover to this day.

- Scotland once ruled over England, Ireland, Wales, and Iceland. It wasn't until Scotland turned its attention to France that England (Sudland, as it was known back then) struck out and, after 3 years of fighting, earned its independence. Within 5 years, Wales and

Scotland were under its rule. Iceland, however, remained untouched.

Tip – Don't get cocky, strike with one lie at a time. Lies are like a house of cards and you mess up once and it is all for nothing. You show patience and you can spend years whispering sweet dishonesties to the same mark. (Just ask my poor friends and family who have patiently endured my deception for years.)

MADE UP MEDICAL FACTS

Ah, any medical lie is the easiest path to walk upon when spreading deceit, for there are always fresh breakthroughs and, besides, how many of us are doctors? Moreover, how many of the doctors are specialists in your chosen field of fabrication? Enjoy this freedom to deceive. However, should you somehow make the unforgivable mistake of delivering a lie in the company of any such individual who calls you on your words – bow out gracefully and memorise their face. Find out everything about them. Know them as well as yourself and, someday, when they're not expecting it, hit them with some magnificent topic they've no idea about. Vengeance is a dish best served chilled to miserable know-it-alls.

P.S. Most doctors hate religion – I have a nice controversial religion section coming up that you can attack them with.

- There are between 12-20 new diseases discovered every year, while only 6-10 cures are found for existing diseases. This is called the "Tempest Effect" and scientists believe every generation brings us closer to a disease capable of wiping out humanity altogether.

- The average size of the penis in a male human being has been grossly misinterpreted and miscalculated in surveys. To get an accurate reading, (as of 2015) the measurements are now measured from tip to shaft only and in fully erect form. Under these guidelines, the average length of an erect penis is 8.2 inches.

- In yoga, the position "downward dog" can be used to relieve a milliard of physical ailments such as chronic hiccups, water knee and long tongue, though, apparently, most doctors don't want you to know this.

- There are actual "love potions" in modern-day medicine. For the moment, these concoctions are perfectly legal yet infrequently used due to their exorbitantly high price and inaccuracy on the intended. A cocktail of synthetic liquid pheromones designed to entice the user's object of affection has revealed startlingly positive results. However, the effect is anything but swift. Moreover, it affects the subconscious once consumed over a manner of days and may last for 2-3 months. Due to this delay, the artificial affections are frequently passed on to an unwitting suitor. Scientists working on this project have admitted to self-medicating themselves (and partners) in attempts to both study at a closer hand the effects, and attempting to "spice up" relationships. This has resulted in tremendous successes but also, unfortunately, divorces after instances of extramarital affairs wherein partners found themselves incredibly attracted to the unintended.

- It is theorised in the medical world that the appendix, once believed to be an unusable organ, will develop further as we evolve. It is further suggested that its function will be capable of tasks akin to both the heart and liver. For this to occur, it is suggested such an evolution would take almost 11 million years.

- Every year, almost 8-9 children are born with what can only be described as extraordinary abilities bordering on the incredible throughout the world, due to kileo- progressive genes. The J'karian test measures the scale of potential in every child born. Though the progress of such abilities is slight to the average person, (12-16% increase in strength or movement speed in most adult cases) to scientists, it is proof that "mutated super humans" may only be a handful of generations away. Alas, the world will still have to wait many years for the first official Superman.

- It is no secret that the average lifespan of human beings is on the rise. In answer to this, so too has the time it has taken for the average human to develop fully. By the year 2,500, it is predicted that, following our current path of advancement within the longevity of our lifespan, an adult human being will not reach full maturity until the age of 40.

- You don't need a medical licence to be a dentist. You do, however, have to pay an entrance fee into dental school and complete 1 year before you are allowed to practice.

- Like the Black Plague gene, all humans carry the Ebola virus and it is suggested that it may be a modern day's way of culling the herd should Mother Nature take a sudden, nasty turn. If the virus ever became airborne, it could wipe out 80% of the world's population in a matter of weeks. With 15% having a natural immunity and a projected 5% or so escaping infection.

- According to the Geralt records, released in 1992 in the United States, there have been 19 genuine cases of E.S.P (Extra Sensory Projection) recorded. 7 of those displayed level three aptitudes such as honing energies and altering objects slightly without touching, whilst 2 subjects further displayed the ability to create a burning flame from behind a lead screen.

- In a medical first, Anzio Boranes was the first and only human ever born with wings in 1889 in Florence, Italy. Medical professionals suggest that these "wings" themselves were defect appendages of thin bone with a fragile membrane which swayed slowly of their own volition, giving the impression of an angel. As a child, he was worshipped among the overtly religious locals and many would travel for miles to touch the swaying wings. As he grew older, the bright skin wings turned an off-black and fell still before slowly withering away due to bad circulation. By his teenage years, he was treated with disdain and was commonly referred to as "demon child." Eventually, in a fit of desperation, he tore them free and though records say he died from shock and blood loss, it is thought his family smuggled him away to a monastery where he became a monk and devoted himself to a life of piety. Regardless, his family line died with him and his grave has never been discovered, much to the irritation of scientists who desire to study a sample of his DNA.

Tip – Whilst there's little point in mastering what clues the average person gives away when lying, a more advanced technique of deceiving is looking to the left when recalling a tall tale. Looking left is what naturally occurs when being truthful as you are accessing the memory of the brain. Looking to the right usually occurs when accessing the more creative segments of the brain. It's where we make the wonderful lies. Who says reading doesn't teach you interesting things?

ENTERTAINMENT ILLUSIONS

What's the best way in the world to get sued? You'd probably suggest kicking a lawyer through a fridge, pouring dog food over their head, while repeatedly chanting that they had no friends in school. There's probably some merit to your answer but it was a rhetorical question. The actual answer is writing a book full of lies about Hollywood shows, movies and stars, and somehow expecting no repercussions. So, with that in mind, THIS IS A BOOK OF LIES AND EVERYTHING IN HERE IS NOT TRUE. Please don't sue me.

- It was the actions of overexcited executives at a prominent television station which resulted in the locating and assassination of Osama bin Laden. Rumours of executives with priceless information involving the whereabouts of the most wanted man in the world began to emerge across the dark net in 2013. The executives in question were proposing a real-time live event, and three stations (and a prominent internet server) had expressed an interest in what may have been the biggest live event of all time. However, with discussions at an early stage, the American government intervened and after agreeing on a compensation package, recovered the information which went on to assist in the successful mission.

- Any workplace is filled with dangers, but to be an extra on a top-end film budget is one of the most dangerous jobs in the world. Approximately 3-6 extras lose their lives in Hollywood every year due to on set accidents. However, in the Indian film industry, the numbers are even higher at 10-20 fatalities on set – the Bollywood universe is precarious at best. To be an extra in the UK and Europe is far safer with only 1-2 approximately losing their lives, though this may be down to the fewer big budgeted movies in production a year.

- The award-winning picture The Shawshank Redemption is actually based on the real-life Andrew DuFresney who was imprisoned in 1923 for murder but escaped without a trace in 1934. However, unlike the movie which suggests heavily of DuFresney's innocence – modern-day investigations suggest not only was he the likely murderer in question, but may have been linked with a spate of murders leading up to his arrest and possibly a further 11 between 1942 and 1957.

- The legendary monster Godzilla of Japanese origin is based on the massive fossils of the Herochiosaur dinosaur whose remains were only found in the Kanto and Chugoku regions. The 12

THE LITTLE BOOK OF LIES

skeletal frames range from 80 meters in height to as high as 150 meters and were believed to walk the earth in the Jurassic period. The second largest dinosaur, the Brachiosaur, stands at a paltry 45 meters at its highest.

- "The Pugilist," is the only pornographic movie to ever be nominated for an academy award in 1972. Public outcry resulted in many nominees boycotting the event which eventually resulted in the withdrawing of the nomination from the best picture and best screenplay categories.

- The first ever movie shown to the Kaibu tribe in 1963 in the central African country of Mombaku was "The Sound of music." It was shown by a group of scientists who wished to study the tribe's unnaturally long life. It was thought the tribe would be amazed by the advancements but it ended with the tribe believing the film to be witchcraft. The scientists were killed and the projector and screen were burned with the bodies, as was the tradition with "demonic activities." It was 1983 before the tribe issued a full apology to the families after a slow integration of modern technology into their culture and a grasp of what motion pictures were.

- The highly rated television show, Supernatural (which follows two demon-hunting brothers in America), deals with adult subject matter interspersed with humour. Even when dealing with fantastical plots and themes, it is quick to poke fun at itself, however, no more so than in the very subtle Easter egg found in every episode since its pilot, where keen-eyed viewers can spot a theatrical figure hiding under a sheet in a comical reference to hunting a ghost. Most of the time they employ a stage hand to conceal themselves in the background but it has become a huge favourite among the fan base.

- Snork the Dork is the longest running cartoon/television show ever. Running from 1922 to 2012 with 22 episodes every season and multiple Christmas specials, there are almost 2,000 episodes; it is unlikely there will ever be a show like it again. Incidentally, its full cast has been replaced at least 3 times over.

- Science Fiction Television Show Babylon 5 is the highest rated show of all time according to ratings on the internet. Alf is second.

- In 1993, a Norwegian television company applied for a licence to show a snuff movie as part of an art piece of cinema history. Needless to say, it was denied the application. The snuff movie in question was never recovered.

Tip – Never lie to cover up another lie no matter what. NO MATTER WHAT! If you are caught in a lie, own it. The more lies in play, the harder it is to escape. This might be good advice for life.

MUSICAL MISDIRECTION

I remember a pretty girl telling me that the reason we like music is because it resonates somewhere in our teeth or some crap like that – I wasn't really interested, I was just trying to build up the courage to ask her out or ask her for other things.

And it's just as well, because I did ask her out and we ended up getting married. Sorry, no, that's a lie. That didn't happen at all. Moreover, I'm fairly certain the nasty witch was lying through her teeth (did you see what I did there?).

Regardless, it's funny how that lie/truth stuck with me for decades. With a bit of luck, you too can place

a delightful little bit of untruth in the mind of a
victim for decades. That's the dream anyway.

- Crowd surfing and mosh pits first began in the
  underground jazz clubs of New York in the early
  1920's. These practices quickly became illegal
  due to injury and rowdiness and it is suggested
  the first stirrings of prohibition began as a way
  of keeping this behaviour in line.

- Rap music was invented in the 1600's by eastern
  European poets. What started as a battle of
  quick-witted poems recited to the beat of a drum
  between feuding poets quickly drew crowds. The
  practice fell out of favour in the early 1900's but
  never died out fully until a renaissance in
  America in the early 80's.

- In a successful attempt at raising money for her charity foundation, Mother Theresa had a number one single in 1983. The song "l'amore e laggiu," (love is over there) was number one in 14 countries simultaneously and raised almost $29 million in record sales. It was rereleased a few months after her death in late 1998 but only made $4 million.

- In 1978, to raise funds for the Ivorian refugees, Elokobi Maluda (of unknown descent) organised a massive charity concert with Africa's biggest performing acts, alongside a selection of international acts. Raising almost 7 million in ticket sales, sponsorship, and charity donations, the massive concert was set to take place on June 11th, 12th, and 13th. Though he'd gone through all the proper channels and booked the land, he did nothing else and instead transferred the funds from all 9 accounts into offshore accounts, two days before the concert. Before authorities could be notified, he fled the country and disappeared into criminal and music folklore forever. Even though word spread of the fraud, almost 4,000 disgruntled fans still turned up to enjoy the silence of an empty field.

- The black note (3-9 Hz below the "brown note" which can bring about involuntary defecation) can slow the heart. It is theorised that, after extended exposure, it may stop the heart altogether. Scientists from the British army have been criticised heavily for conducting extensive experiments in the field.

- The musical instrument, the triangle, has 47 different tones in the hands of a master.

- Best friends, Ludwig van Beethoven and Wolfgang Amadeus Mozart, were the original hell raisers in their day. It wasn't just their music which earned them  such fame in Vienna. They were known to enjoy lengthy salacious nights with varied groups of female companions, fuelled on by copious amounts of alcohol and recreational drugs of the time. It wasn't a rare occurrence for both to show up at each other's performances completely inebriated whilst the other was barely able to stand upright at the podium. All while their entourage took the best podium seats, much to the chagrin of the wealthier patrons and sometimes royals. Eventually, the owners of the concert halls left a balcony empty every night in the event of rowdy entourage. It wasn't until Mozart died from suspected alcohol poisoning that Beethoven tapered his ways. However, by then, he had lost his sense of hearing due to the years of abuse.

- Norwegian Black Metal is played loudly in Alpine regions by Swiss rangers to dislodge unstable areas of snow in the hope of avoiding devastating avalanches. It is estimated that the music saves hundreds of lives every year.

- Iconic funk band "The Hop Step n'Jumps" are the first band to ever record an album in space. Recorded in 2014 in the international space station over a three-week period, the 47 mins album "Songs from a Funkier Earth" sold 70,000 copies which failed to cover the cost of producing the album. Not to be undone, they have recorded 3 new songs from a deep submersible and are intending to be the first band to record an album from the bottom of the earth's ocean.

- 147 people died at Woodstock from drug overdoses.

Tip – Maintaining eye contact when lying is total balderdash but sometimes it's best to stick with what is traditionally perceived to be the truth. "Look me in the eye and say that," as the old movie saying goes. Well, you should look them right in the eye and gleefully lie through your teeth.

PEOPLE'S PORKY PIES

Hey, you in the bookstore. Buy this book right now!

Right, so, halfway through the book. Statistically speaking, this is the likeliest page a casual browser in a bookshop will open. So, hey, casual shopper, how's your day going? Aha…yes…well, that's very interesting…and I don't actually care. You see, I'm just trying to win you over by feigning interest so you will give me money and I may buy food for my cat. He's a big cat. That was a lie. I don't have a cat. I have a drug problem. Anyway, I like money and people are a joy to lie about. So much so that I've had to cut quite a number from this section. The best lies I've saved for the sequel and if that sequel is sitting beside this one on the shelf of the bookstore, go to page 69. I've left you a message. Also, I do have a cat and I'm managing the drug habit.

- Abraham Lincoln is portrayed as a giant man in more ways than one. Though his legacy as a leader can never be questioned, his actual appearance differs. History portrays him as a tall man but, in fact, this couldn't be further from the truth. Standing at a meagre 4 ft 10 inches, he resorted to standing on raised podiums when addressing crowds. The famed sugar hat he wore was another tool he used to give the appearance of being taller than he really was.

- Hitler spent his youth as a struggling comedian in the Austrian city of Vienna before World War One. Though his brand of comedy involved thinly disguised racist slurs and an overreliance on the use of props, he did sharpen his skills at engaging hostile crowds.

- Sun Tzu was a famed tactician and author of the wildly influential military strategy book "The Art of War." However, little is known of the general apart from the fact that he was of African descent and once he reached his twentieth year, he resigned his commission to live a quieter life away from war and death.

- The old farmer, Izidiel, is the first recorded man to milk a cow according to early writings. Working his failing farm during a famine in 12,000 B.C, he had one cow to his name and barely anything else. Paying with the shirt off his back and most of his food stocks, he had his cow mate with a neighbouring farmer's bull. The calf was born weak and fed on its mother's teat. He noticed the cow moaned in pain until the calf fed. But as the days passed, the calf grew weaker and eventually died. A pack of wolves sensing the meal stole the body in the night, leaving Izidiel with nothing at all. Days passed and Izidiel grew hungry. The cow lamented like nothing he'd ever heard before until he realised what was causing the beast so much pain. After three days and nights without rest, listening to its cries, he tended to the beast as a calf would. He drained the milk into a pitcher until the crying ceased and, crazed with hunger, he drank from the pitcher, found sustenance, and survived the famine. Moreover, he found eventual wealth in selling pails of milk.

- Shakespeare is a pseudo name. The Shaking Spears trio were a comedy group from Ireland who achieved fame throughout London. When one of their main writers, Michael O'Shaughnessy, attempted to steer their plays from comedy, the group went into turmoil and eventually split. Only Michael continued to write under the moniker The Shaking Spear. Eventually, he became known as Michael Shakespeare. Until simply Shakespeare. In Ireland, O'Shaughnessy day is celebrated every August 18th.

- South African man, Terence Wister, is the first man to suffer from Columbidae Infectious syndrome. This is an overwhelming attraction to pigeons. In 2003, he applied and was granted a marriage certificate to a pigeon, however, in 2004, he applied for and was granted a full annulment citing abandonment and non-consummation of marriage after the pigeon flew off a few weeks into their married life.

- Before his life as a legendary leader and instrument of peace, Mahatma Gandhi was an amateur boxer with a record of 15-3-2, however, before he could qualify outright for the Olympic Games, he was shrouded in an irregular betting scandal and pulled out of the trials amid public outcry.

- Napoleon Bonaparte, the famed war general, is a true example of history being written by the victors. Despite his legacy as an indomitable force, his skills as a leader were sorely overrated. When he rose to leader of the French army, he introduced conscription and, within 4 months, his army outnumbered all others by almost 10 soldiers to 1. With such swelling numbers in the ranks, he marched across

Germany, the Netherlands, and many parts of England before returning home and declaring himself King of France. However, during the French revolution, he was the first ever man to lose his head to the guillotine followed quickly by his wife, Marie Antoinette.

- Cleopatra was voted into power by election but died before she could finish her first year in term. Her legacy as a great beauty lives on but it is suggested she was anything but. Statues recovered suggest she was wealthy, middle-aged, obese, and simply paid artists and sculptors to depict her as a ravishing beauty during and after the elections. It is also suggested it was a heart attack which claimed her life and not an asp.

- Jack the Ripper was not actually a man, or indeed a sole killer. There is resounding proof that the killer who stalked London prostitutes during the 1800's was actually a group of women hell-bent on cornering the prostitution business for themselves.

- **Harry Houdini and Charley Chaplin were the same person. When the escapist illusions began to wane in popularity, under the suggestion of his agent, he changed his name to avoid the typecasting involved in his name.**

- Julius Caesar didn't exist. Julies Caesar was the first female Caesar of Rome and was widely regarded as both a popular and successful leader. In her decade-long reign, she conquered Gaul, Germanica and reimagined the road system which spread throughout Europe and brought great prosperity to a city facing ruination. Her name was changed after her death by her political opposition, who belittled her successes as a way to disempower women throughout the empire. There are still gold pieces in museums which bear her name, title, and resemblance.

- Dave Kinsky is the first man to be sucked into a class F5 hurricane and survive to tell the tale. Back in 2011, while flying his glider across the outskirts of Wichita in the state of Kansas, he inadvertently flew into the massive tornado as it formed and blew east. Miraculously enough, after fighting the winds for a few minutes without having his glider fall apart, he was sucked up through the funnel where he lost consciousness. His video camera caught the terrifying ordeal where twenty minutes after the event, he woke up almost 7000 feet up, passing over Missouri almost 100 miles away.

- Karl Shlager suffered from one of the stranger phobias in recorded history. The German national feared cold hands so much that he kept a pair of gloves on his person at all times. Ever since he was a child, he insisted on buying a new pair of gloves or mittens whenever he could. Not only that, but this phobia grew as he got older and by the age of 40 (despite being happily married with children), he was spending almost $5,000 a year adding to his collection. This phobia soon spread from himself to those he was closest to. When his family awoke one summer morning to mittens on each of their hands, he finally agreed to counselling. Eventually, he overcame his phobia and turned his nightmares into profit by setting up the National Mittens & Gloves Museum in Dusseldorf. Remarkably enough, he has amassed millions of visitors to his museum over the last decade.

- "7 Fingers Fritz" is a 1920's blues guitarist considered to be the finest musician to ever live. Due in part to 7 fingers on his left hand and 6 fingers on his right. Sadly, he was underappreciated while alive and died a pauper, but his records went on to sell over 20 million since his death in 1931 from consumption.

- Da Vinci's last words were a confession. "This great mind is not my own. These thoughts were from the stolen book of Siensta. Forgive my life." As there is no written record of the individual "Siensta" anywhere in Italian written history, historians believe Siensta was the nickname he gave to his master, Maciennes, who he studied under as a precocious ten-year-old. His master died a pauper when he was 12 years old but his works were never recovered which was rare for a renowned artist and inventor in that period.

Tip – If a mark calls you on your lie, shrug and suggest they look it up online sometime. When they go to take out their phone, gently insist looking up things on the internet among company is considered rude and resist the urge to check your own phone for the rest of the night.

SCIENTIFICAL SOUNDING STATEMENTS

I was lying before; I deliberately left out any lies on any religions. In truth, to lie about something as precious as religion among people is precarious at best and I recommend wholeheartedly that you avoid this practice as much as possible. It's just not worth the trouble you'll find yourself in.

Even though this book is certainly meant to deceive, I have little intention of insulting or offending people. Apart from Nazis. **Nazis have really stupid haircuts.** Anyway, instead of religion, I decided to put in its counter opposite. Science!

Scientific lies are the trickiest lies to create yet the easiest to make believable. You can say almost anything and people will assume it's completely true.

- As of 2014, 43% of geographical scientists believe the core of the planet Earth is actually ocean. The magma layer is a thin membrane no more than 3 kilometres at its deepest. Many refer to the water as the "Sea of Ailedroc" and 16% believe there to be any life forms capable of surviving in such inhospitable conditions.

- The colour whiter than white comes from the compound Phosphoroun, which has such a glaringly bright whiteness, it has been suggested that extended exposure to it causes headaches and can cause short-term memory loss.

- Up to as recently as 9 million years ago, flowers emitted deadly toxins to keep predators at bay, including human beings. However, as we advanced, the toxins became less toxic, and then manageable, until they eventually became alluring to our senses.

- Clouds are in decline. Since 1987, cloud cover around the world has decreased by almost 12 sikilo tonnes a month because of the greenhouse effect and increases in acid rainfall.

- Due to global warming, grass is slowly changing colour from rich green to an off-yellow. On a molecular yellow, the toxins in the air have affected the pigmentation in 3% of grassland across the northern hemisphere already and it is theorised that by 2050, the phrase "the grass is always yellower on the other side of the fence," will be the more common term.

- Rifts in time and space are common enough occurrences under specific experimentation, but harnessing any such events  is an impossible task. Through the use of a supercollider, it is possible to pass an inanimate  object through a rift. However, any accurate control of its destination or reappearance has proven to be difficult but scientists still continue to experiment.

- The earth is slowly revolving away from our sun. At some point within the next 250 thousand years, it is believed that it (and the moon) may slip away from the sun's gravity completely where the earth will no longer be considered a planet but a self-sustaining asteroid.

- In specific points of latitude and longitude on earth, it is possible to leap in the air and remain airborne for 7% longer than anywhere else due to a drop in the earth's gravitational pull. Because of this natural phenomenon, any sporting events or records broken in these specific regions are completely unsanctioned by any sporting bodies.

- We are all slightly colour blind and the sky isn't blue. To be more exact, the colour of the sky that we perceive isn't actually blue. It is grey but our eyes are unable to focus that particular shade unless viewed through a specific set of lenses which display colours in their natural state. Incidentally, 1% of the population are able to see the natural colour unaided.

- For 2 decades, food synthesisers akin to science fiction television shows are a reality. I.e. a simple request to a computer results in instantaneously prepared food, ready for consumption. When asking for a particular dish, the revolutionary prototype machine named the "Real-insta-meal," is capable of producing any flavour of meal in almost 9 seconds, using quick-boil water, raw proteins, and combining an array of pre-set infused flavourings. Though the flavour for almost 3000 meals have already been programmed into the machine, only the basics of substance are available as of 2017. Namely, more substantial meals are only available in a brown gelatinous state; however, any soup or broth is completely indiscernible from a traditionally prepared meal.

Tip – Always agree with someone's scepticism when telling a lie. "I know it's absolutely crazy" is a wonderful choice of words mid-lie to add weight to the utter rubbish coming out of your mouth. You might even begin with "This is a crazy thing I heard the other day." It immediately opens their mind to the fantastical.

SEXY SHENANIGANS

Kids, you really shouldn't lie. Lying is really bad. Even white ones – but if you insist on lying, you may as well become a talented one. So, congratulations on this wonderful path you have chosen. Now, skip this chapter and come back to it when you are older.

Right, so now that they're out of the way, we can delve into the juicy stuff, so to speak. Whilst creating this book, I had to do quite a lot of research on various subjects. You would be surprised how many "lies" turn out to be actual "truths." So, with that in mind, I needed to be quite thorough in my research and queries and…ahem…online searches.

After an exhausting journey into the lusciously salacious world of decadence, (where even my internet provider emailed me at one point to ask about my mental health, and if there was someone I needed to talk to or just if I needed a hug) I bring you the sexiest of all lies.

- In one of the many islands off the Portuguese region of Dellerin, the inhabitants have a more liberal approach to sexual activities. With a population of almost 120,000 people, their culture from the age of 18 onwards venerates sexual relations at a far more casual level. Sex is frequently shared between willing partners and considered little more than a courteous act between acquaintances. In some extreme cases, it can be a form of greeting, while in others, a carefree way to alleviate the tribulations of the day. There is no greater honour than taking the virginity of a lover. Special mention goes to the act of offering a husband or wife to a guest. Though attraction DOES frequently come in to the act, attraction between parties is not necessary. In fact, to take a lover with lower attraction is considered a thing of pride. Incidentally, due to the practice of safe sex, the spread of sexual diseases is lower than in neighbouring regions and sexual crimes are the lowest in the world.

- The first sexual aids using vibration as a form of pleasure for females were first used by the ruling class in ancient Egypt. Queens and nobles would store scores of locusts in a wafer-thin wooden tube lined with agave juice called "the Percusser." The insects frenzy with the juice and cause the tube to vibrate. Afterwards, the locusts are released to a cage and kept in storage for when needed next.

- Lettuces were used by males as a tool for sexual pleasure and for practicing both cunnilingus and penetration on forthcoming brides. This was crudely referred to as "tasting the delicious, bitter greens."

- Incest between homosexual brothers is legal in the majority of countries of the world.

- Bilsiem Monks are an isolated sect of religious men in Belgium, capable of producing a pheromone which can entice a woman (and man where desired) to their bed. Through deep meditation and after many years of training their bodies to react to certain emotions, test subjects have admitted to frequently finding themselves increasingly aroused the longer they stay in the monastery as guests. Incidentally enough, the monks are not required to live a life of celibacy. There are dormitories provided for both male and female guests throughout the year. It is reported that there are few days where there are free beds. Donations towards continuation of their lifestyle are usually made on departure from the monastery.

- In recent surveys, 91% of males have admitted to attempting oral sex on themselves on more than one occasion. 36% of females have also attempted fellatio more than once.

- "High hopes" by Frank Zappa and "Everything is alright" by Army of Ed, have been voted as the most seductive pieces of music when attempting coitus with a lover.

- In the Zibabwa Coast in Africa, it is illegal to perform oral sex between heterosexual couples unless full penetration occurs thereafter. It is, however, allowed between same-sex partners as the creation of children is not a factor.

- In a recent poll, American heterosexual couples average their love making to be between 1-3 hours. Same-sex couples almost twice as long.

- An inebriated man was once arrested for attempting oral pleasure from a blowfish in a pet shop in Devon, Scotland. On three separate occasions, in one afternoon, the man attempted to remove the fish from its tank before horrified staff intervened and, eventually, police arrested him for public indecency.

- 88% of happily married couples swap partners at least once in their marriage. Many experts say this is a major reason couples maintain a healthy sexual relationship.

- Almost 20% of unisex bathrooms in Europe and Asia contain Glory holes.

Tip – Never be afraid to back down if you are caught out, but as you do, pretend that it was always your plan to back down. If there is no way out of the lie, stop and immediately agree with the accuser. A skilled deceiver might even feign gratitude and act humble, thus completely throwing off the accuser, e.g. "Thank you, I was thinking the same thing, I just knew it couldn't be true." You might even go on about how it's impossible to read the truth these days. The true Machiavellian amongst you may go one step further and blame the lie on a mutual acquaintance. "Larry said it to me last week – I really hate Larry."

SPORTY STORIES

Warning – this is without a doubt the most
dangerous of all type of lies to strike with. No matter
what table or group you are out with, there is always
a high chance that someone with a greater bout of
sporting knowledge will be hovering near you.
Moreover, there is also the horrific chance that
NOBODY in the immediate vicinity cares about
sport! I mean, really, what type of existence is that?
Anyway, there is nothing more upsetting in the
world than saying "Blah, blah was actually a
professional graffiti artist before they signed a
multimillion deal for blah, blah sports team at 14
years old" and your audience smiles weakly, eyes

the door and says, "that's very interesting" while trying to conceal the derision in their tones. There's no coming back from that. NO COMING BACK! So, take care with this one.

- In the Tour de France, drug tests are optional on the higher climbs and all sections after the third day, due to the excessive amounts of stress already put on the athletes' bodies. Urine and blood samples are posted out to the authorities before and after events to ensure fairness and transparency is shared between all participating athletes.

- In 1918, the English footballer and previous season's top scorer, Gerry Swinton, signed for Aldershot Rovers from Liverpool FC in the old English league, for a then transfer fee of £180 pounds. At the time, the player's value was 17 times the actual value of the club. The club incurred devastatingly high debt on the bank loan in the belief that the player would earn the club a first ever league title and the debt could be subsidised by success on the field. The gamble began as a success and the club won the 1918-1919 league title, despite the tepid season from its star player. Scoring only 6 times in 42 games, the player became a character of ridicule in front of his home supporters and was eventually sold back to Liverpool FC a year later, for a measly £10 where he returned to his scoring ways. Liverpool FC went on to tremendous success winning the league a historic five seasons in a row while Aldershot Rovers were relegated in 1921, and eventually were liquidated in 1923. When their stadium was knocked down to make way for a housing estate in 1929, they named the area "Swinton's close."

- The oldest ever basketball player in the NBA is hall of famer Chuck "Downtown" O'Neal of the Kansas Stars. Born in 1880, he played in the 1949 season at the ripe old age of 69. Having played independent basketball for almost 40 years, standing at a colossal 7ft 8 inches and blessed with exceptional ball skills, he was frequently used as the team's point guard. Sadly, in his second season in the warm-up before a playoff game, he fell suddenly ill and died a few days later. Since his demise, the fledgling NBA (still finding its feet as a legitimate organisation) had to enforce strict rules that no player may compete beyond the age of 50.

- Heroin used to be used as a performance-enhancing drug in the 1950's by boxers hoping to make weight. It also assisted with increasing the pain threshold in bouts until outlawed completely in the mid 70's.

- Baseball is "America's Game" but it was actually invented in Canada and is still their 5th chosen sport.

- "Avalanche riding" originated in northern Austria and is growing in popularity among extreme sports enthusiasts, despite its illegality. It involves controlled explosions in segregated sections of the Saalbach mountain region to bring about an unnatural avalanche where snowboarders ride the resulting surging snow down the mountainside. There are fatalities recorded every year of those engaging in this sport.

- Russia, China, and America have jointly submitted a request for future Olympic Games to allow the use of performance-enhancing drugs in all events.

- In the 1930's, Formula 1 drivers' mortality rate was so high that many of the top teams had up to 6 different drivers employed in each team despite only running two cars per race. Unsuitable track surfaces and inadequately protected fencing, not to mention untested engines, were responsible. It was only after the "Black Blurnburg Weekend" in Germany in 1937 in which 7 drivers were fatally wounded over the course of 3 days that the first safety regulations were brought in.

- Ricardo "Junk box" Speroni was an Italian-American middleweight boxing champion during the great depression in New York. His record of 147-0 cements him as the greatest champion of all time with 59 world title defences. However, because boxing was not accurately regulated until 1921 (when the WBA came into effect), his official record was 21-0 before he perished in a house fire at the tender age of 27.

- Ice hockey legend, Arnie Chatosky, was the starting goalkeeper for the Montreal Moose in 1955 and not only finished the season with the league's most shutouts (15), but was also top scorer with 81 points due to his tendency to stray out and attack.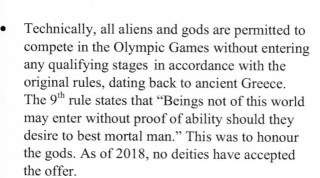

- Technically, all aliens and gods are permitted to compete in the Olympic Games without entering any qualifying stages in accordance with the original rules, dating back to ancient Greece. The 9th rule states that "Beings not of this world may enter without proof of ability should they desire to best mortal man." This was to honour the gods. As of 2018, no deities have accepted the offer.

Tip – If you spot someone doubting your words, you would be surprised how mid-sentence, simply telling them "no, no, this is true" works to sell the lie. People desire the strange and ludicrous. They want to believe you. Idiots.

UNEXPLAINED UNSETTLING UNTRUTHS

Oh, these lies are the most fun to whisper when dealing with a mark who has a nervous disposition. If you play it right, you can give nightmares to those closest to you. What's more, you can do so on more than one occasion. It really only takes an unsettling lie to ruin someone's day. Another note to remember is the mark will NEVER read up about these lies. The unexplained lies might be the closest thing to the perfect crime. So, seek out your victim and watch the colour drain from their face as you unnerve them ever so.

- Every year (since 1979), on March 10th at exactly 11.58 am GMT, a radio signal is received across the northern hemisphere at the frequency 18.37 MW. This signal originates from a dwarf cluster at the edge of the Andromeda Galaxy. It repeats itself for exactly 73 mins. The interspersed signals are of no known cypher and repeated attempts by the earth's top cryptographers to discover the message have ended in failure. The closest suggested message is "Peace of" in ancient Sumerian, though other scientists believe it is simply a delayed release of gamma rays from a dead star causing interference.

- In 210 BC, numerous scrolls spoke of a terrifying object or vessel large enough to block out the light of the sun and the moon as it moved slowly across the sky. "A god's chariot of fire and bronze looked upon us for a day and a night and, throughout the land, we shook as it passed." And again in 890 AD, the same descriptions were given in many different locations all across the world, including paintings by Native Americans and Australian aborigines suggesting this was no eclipse.

- Ever since 1979 to present day, all across America, countless children have spoken of their imaginary friend named "Chillsie." No scientists or psychologists can explain why this phenomenon (or why the imaginary friend in question) only ever resembles a pig-human hybrid. The most notable similarities are that when further studied, the children only ever stated "Chillsie did it" when discovered "misbehaving" and relentlessly insisting "Chillsie doesn't like mommy and daddy," when asked what Chillsie was thinking at any given moment.

- Enormous designs in both the Saharan and Atacama Desert have mystified scientists in recent years. Ever since Google maps took photographs from satellites, strange objects have been discovered but none more so than the newly discovered desert designs. Spanning as big as 300 miles across and 300 miles deep, these elaborate shapes resemble crop circles but on a far grander scale. It's almost impossible to see the designs from the ground due to their scale and resemble nothing more than slight indents and rises in the ground. Moreover, two years after the first set of photos were taken, a second set have revealed fresh designs, disproving the suggestion it was the cause of erratic winds over many years.

- H.P. Lovecraft swore to the bitter end that the creatures and worlds he wrote about were real. "The dark one is still knocking, closer now," were his last words. After his death, among his notes were random scribblings theorising how to open "doors" into alternate dimensions using unconventional theories and sketches of peculiar machines still too advanced in this modern age. His notes are not only relevant today, but also many of his equations have proven invaluable to scientists and have driven the possibility of interdimensional travel forwards. As for the "Dark One", his writings suggest this is Cthulhu.

- "Azel the Movie" is an infamous 1970's low budget horror film famed for its curse. It follows the urban legend of the half-demon, Azel, who allegedly butchered over a hundred women in the 12th century in Romania. On set, the production was plagued with strange accidents, including the director of photography's drowning, when a camera unit slid off a riverbank and trapped him beneath the water. The lead writer committed suicide a week into production and the director and main lead were diagnosed with terminal cancer in the latter few weeks of filming. By its final release, there was already a cult following, but with 2 cinemas inexplicitly burning down in its opening weekend due to the cheaper volatile reels used, expected attendances were catastrophically lower than usual. The film house who released the picture went out of business within 18 months of release and 11 members from crew and cast passed away within ten years of the movie's release. As if to remind the film world of its unsettling curse, in 2003, it was released on DVD, and in reply, a mudslide tore through the town from where the legend originated and killed a dozen people that very day.

- In the region around Loch
  Ness, tourists (usually
  backpackers) frequently
  disappear without a trace.
  This trend first began in
  1845 when records of
  missing locals began to appear. Between 1845
  and 1930, there were on average 2-3 people
  reported missing every year. By 1940, that
  number had doubled and again in 1978, the
  numbers reached as much as ten people going
  missing. However, in 1986, inexplicitly the
  numbers dropped back to 1-2 missing persons.
  Radical monster hunters claim this suggests that
  "Nessie" mated and either the offspring died or
  else moved to a neighbouring lake. As of 2018,
  there have been no further changes in
  disappearances, though visitors are warned
  against venturing out into the moorlands at night
  unaccompanied.

- Ruins of an Incan architecture were discovered
  in the Arctic in 1942. The solitary structure

stands exactly 15ft in height and exactly 15ft across. The walls are made from 35 marble slabs considered too precisely cut by hand with tools from their time. The stone is also considered impossibly heavy for any seafaring of that time. There is a spire which points skywards and archaic hieroglyphics suggesting a countdown to some unknown event. However, the timing is indecipherable as the primary date has been worn away by corrosion. To this day, it has baffled archaeologists and scientists as to its purpose but chaos theorists are happy to declare it to be a countdown to an apocalyptic event.

- The American civil war raged on for 6 months more than expected, down to the strange stories of General Chester Peterson rallying the beaten south in certain battles. It is suggested that he appeared on the eve of defeat and rallied beaten southern soldiers. What should have been relatively straightforward victories for the North turned into prolonged costly skirmishes which sapped advancement and led to far greater casualties on both sides. There are no records of the general's career from before or indeed after, save for his sudden emergence at the end of the war through one solitary reference of his name and various battle journals. It was his theatrical appearance of donning a cloak of fire and armed with a battle scythe instead of traditional sabre which set him apart from more conventional leaders. "He roared loudly and the trees seemed to sway in his wake. The ground shook as he charged and we turned from our retreat and charged with him. With the smell of sulphur in our noses, we searched for death and we died when we could have lived, but it didn't matter. He laughed as he raged into the northern fools and took many of their heads with one swipe. It was beautiful and bloody until there were too few of us to hold the line and then he was gone, and he took our nerve with him." – An extract taken from a soldier's journal at the battle of Wolfen Valley.

- On Christmas Day in 1972 in Quiet Lake, Arkansas, a family of 9 disappeared without a trace from the family farm. The bodies were never discovered but every floor of every room was covered in dried blood. The front and back doorknobs were both burned and melted away. The disappearance of an entire herd of cattle from their secured pen just added to the mystery. The official police reports state, "Cattle rustling turned to murder when discovered" but what is most unsettling is that there are records of snowfall in that area from the night before yet there were no footprints near the house or indeed near the livestock pens.

Tip – Most people smile when they are caught telling humorous lies. So, practice frowning if an accusation comes your way. And you SHOULD frown if people are calling shenanigans a little too frequently, because you are obviously doing it wrong.

VIDEO GAME GRIEVANCES

It was always going to be difficult to invent lies
about the video games world because said world is
already littered with blatant lies from all quarters,
not to mention the most vicious of all our troll
brethren. In fact, much of the world's trolling
problems can be traced back to early internet video
game sites where aggression and venom first
sprouted its fangs. Ah, where have the years gone?
Anyway, it really is very difficult to stand out as an
accomplished deceiver in this area, but at least you
will have the advantage of being capable of lying to
someone in person as opposed to hiding behind a
keyboard and spouting outrage.

- Tetris was originally called "Tetnis" and involved the blocks forming a defensive wall against infection in the body. When the creator of the game was told the true spelling of the word Tet-an-us, he returned with its new title and altered the gameplay to suit the new style. It went on to become the most popular game of all time.

- Fifa football and John Madden games all originally ran off the same "Barbie Dreamland" engine. One of Electronic Arts' first endeavours was the now-defunct Barbie series. The Barbie dreamland engine was created in the late 80's with the intent of taking advantage of the Barbie doll phenomenon sweeping the nation. The franchise ceased after the second instalment ("Barbie and Ken's wild' n wet adventures") failed to break the projected 69,000 units sold. However, the impressive tech used in the original John Madden series was kept. Though Electronic Arts frequently rename their current engine as a strong marketing tool, the tech is still lifted from the original build. It is, however, referred to as the "BD" engine.

- The acclaimed Grand Theft Auto series was originally a homemade top down board game played by dev's in between coding marathons to ease tension and create camaraderie. "Imagine if we put this into a game" was a running joke in their offices until, during a lull in business, they created a demo involving an aggressive ginger-haired soldier breaking into barber shops and stealing black/blonde/brown hair dye while avoiding the "hair police." As development progressed, they followed the more traditional rules of the board game until they began to publish the idea with a workable demo.

- World of Warcraft 2 has declined in popularity since its troubled release, so much so that concurrent users at a midweek low have maxed out at 1837 users. However, the original World of Warcraft still has a concurrent user base of 250,000 on a daily basis.

- ## Pac man started out as an antivirus program.

- Final Fantasy was supposed to be a standalone title. Its creator based the entire premise on this strategy at a time when Japanese role-playing games were growing in popularity in western culture, and watered-down sequels to his favourite games were flooding the market and diminishing their predecessor's legacy. Since its inception, there have been 19 sequels, 43 spin offs, 14 remakes and 73 iOS titles so far.

- In Zibabwa, 15% of military training budget is spent on high-end computers and virtual reality units for specialist soldiers to hone their skills in combat. Using popular first-person shooters, the special forces units train for anywhere up to 8 hours a day and have earned renown throughout the African nations as the most lethal and formidable special forces unit.

- In French schools, Mario Kart is used in simulation booths to instruct children from 9 years old once a week as part of their education. It is believed such sessions have increased reflexes and awareness and serve the children well when they take their full driving test at 13 years old. Incidentally, car collisions involving minors have dropped by 43% since 1997.

- In 2015, an experiment involving a dozen chimpanzees and Halo was conducted. After instruction and months of local play amongst each other and the scientists, the primates learned the complex manoeuvres of the game and, in one spectacular instance, one of the chimpanzees (under the Xbox live tag "banana_1837") finished as high as 4th in a 16-player match online. As of 2018 and under supervision, the chimpanzees still play as a clan, however, their tags and clan name are closely guarded secrets.

- # Bingo Dreams 3 was the first game to go platinum in 1988 and cleared the way for multiplayer game modes.

- In 2002, Pro Evolution Soccer 1 was originally one part of a multimode sports simulation game for the Tokyo Olympic Games. Early builds had the "Soccer" section of the game surpassing the other 32 events in playability, performance, and entertainment which led to the designers ceasing development on the other events altogether to focus on the soccer elements. They released the game as a standalone title at the end of the year to grand acclaim. Like Fifa, the original title still keeps the early build on its engine so it was possible to play the other 31 events (albeit in a very basic format) in every iteration up to Pro Evolution Soccer 2014.

- It's no surprise to learn that many football teams use the incredible database of Football Manager as a means of assisting in scouting players, however, more and more top-flight teams are releasing their scouts altogether and using the database instead. As of 2017, there are now only 3 scouts employed at Premier League teams.

- There's no regulation on age certification in Tasmania, so most development companies with a potential R rating game beta test their games in that region. In fact, 29% of employment growth has been attributed to beta testing in the last ten years. Incidentally, there has been a severe drop in gun crime throughout the region in recent years.

- When Minecraft was first developed, its developers shopped the demo around to many major studios in the hope of publishing.

However, over 15 studios turned down the game outright. Instead of giving up, the development team turned to crowdfunding and the game became an instant hit upon release.

- Player Unknown's Battlegrounds' first map "Erangel" is based accurately upon the county (state) of "Kildare" in Ireland, from where Player Unknown hails. The second map "Miramar" was designed by him and his young daughter in her sandbox using a stick to draw out the map.

- Because of the heated rivalry in the early 90's between Sega and Atari, there were frequent fistfights between 2 rival gangs of game fans throughout Tokyo. Eventually, on February 15th, the scuffles took a nasty turn when on the eve of the release of Atari's spring sale, a large group of Sega fans fell upon the waiting crowd, including the rival gang, outside The Electronics Boutique. On both sides, 7 people in total died during the clashes. Afterwards, a truce was called which still stands today.

Tip – Don't be afraid to throw in a few titbits of truth in between lies. A true master is not afraid to tell the truth 90% of the time and occasionally drop in a mammoth mistruth. It is all part of the long game.

WAR WRONGNESS

Still haven't sorted that whole alphabet crap yet. It's fine, I'm almost done with these introductions anyway so I'm not really trying anymore and, besides, I'm hungry and the cat wants to go out. He's a bit of an idiot. It's raining and he'll just be back at the door in a few minutes. He's actually a dog. Anyway, because it's been running through my head, I'll say it first, WAR! What is it good for? Absolutely nothing, except lies. Yep, I'll get my coat.

- The fateful order for the invasion of Normandy during the Second World War ended with the eventual road to victory against the German army. However, things could have been very different if the delayed plans of "hold for the season and dig in along the coast" were received 6 hours before landfall. As it was, due to a chance-bombing run by German bombers cut off a communications line, the orders never came through and the attacks went ahead as planned. It is theorised that had the allies held off due to the possibility of adverse weather conditions, the Germans may have reached 4 pinnacle strongholds along the French coast which may well have stemmed the allies' joint effort.

- On the night of June 5th, 1986, tensions between the United States and the USSR were at an all-time high, so high in fact that it spread into space. The US space shuttle "Endeavour" while finishing its routine orbit strayed into Russian air space. Subsequently, the vessel came under fire from the Mir space station, to which after repeatedly issuing attempts at communicating, the Endeavour returned fire. However, only fitted with 12 mm cannons, the counter attacks were largely ineffective. For 3-5 minutes, both exchanged fire until the Endeavour suffered catastrophic failures. Issuing one last plea, the Mir space station broke protocol, ceased their barrage, and came to the rescue of the shuttle. Most historians agree this event led the way for the eventual warming of the cold war.

- Glow sticks were invented in the 60's by the British army to assist SAS Special Forces during night skirmishes. It was proposed that the glow sticks would be beneficial in underwater and night missions in keeping visual contact with each other. Unfortunately, the SAS's success rate dropped significantly and the project was scrapped completely. It was only in the late 80's that glow sticks became public domain.

- The Irish Army still have a Spud Gun regiment, though they are little more than ceremonial in modern-day warfare. The last time the regiment were implemented into active duty was during the May Day riots of 1995 wherein they received both criticism and commendation for crowd control.

- Late on in World War 2, the Nazis finally invented the "Panzertwaffte" which was a tank capable of flight. With a V2 rocket assisting and compensating for the additional weight in flight and shielding too thick to be penetrated by traditional firepower – historians and military strategists both agree that had the plane been finished 6-8 months earlier in the war, the outcome may have been quite different. As it was, there were only a dozen of these weapons created, though even in the latter weeks of the war, they inflicted devastating damage to the allies steamrolling advancement through Germany.

- At the beginning of World War 2, Germany annexed Poland but at a terrible price. At the cost of almost 3 million German soldiers and almost 4 bloody years of fighting. By the time France fell, the German army was significantly weakened.

- According to the national budget, the United States defence department have a response unit in the unlikely event of a class 1, 2 and 3, zombie outbreak, though funding is limited to 65 million dollars, making it the lowest funded of all defence departments.

- The French were the first
  army to use fireworks in
  open warfare. During the
  Sudanese incursions of the
  late 1700's, they bombarded
  different settlements with 3

  ½ tonnes of the inexpensive materials, which
  served as a way of spreading both mayhem and
  fear among the rebelling villagers who had never
  seen fire displayed in such a way. By the second
  night of bombardment, they offered a complete
  surrender. Despite the effectiveness without the
  loss of lives, they were swiftly replaced by the
  use of gunpowder with rifles and cannons.

- The Great Latin American war between Brazil
  and a coalition of Argentina/Columbia/Peru and
  Bolivia between 1767 and 1769 is considered
  one of the bloodiest wars ever. Clashes between
  the two armies resulted in almost 2 million
  fatalities. Eventually, due to Spain and
  Portugal's intervention, an uneasy truce was

drawn up with no outright winner. This truce still stands to this day.

- There was a third nuclear bomb dropped in Japan in the city of Kokura three days after the Nagasaki bombing. However, an error in its assembly resulted in a non-detonation. The bomb was recovered 2 months after Japan surrendered and disposed of it. It is theorised 150,000 people may have perished in the bombing had it been successful.

Tip – If you become known as a "liar" or a "bit of a storyteller" among friends, comrades, or workmates, this book is no good to you at all. Give it all up this very moment and begin a pilgrimage of truthfulness, for at least a decade or so. (Or at least until people learn to trust you once more.) Until then, lock this book away in a safe and when the time comes, it will be waiting for you.

ONE LINER LIES

A great one-liner is where it all begins. There are few details to learn, and with one breath and an excellent delivery, you may cause absolute devastation. This is where I finish the book, but this is where you begin your glorious journey towards a life of delicious dishonesty. For those of you who are unsure of your fledgling ability, begin with these little pieces of magic. Practice, practice, practice. Hone your delivery on these until perfect, and soon enough, you will find yourself listing off the untruths like a Master.

- Snails and slugs are technically part of the reptile family and are classified as snakes.

- Marie Antoinette founded the French Revolution. Later, she became France's first President.

- Flies can bite and are responsible for spreading Ebola throughout African countries.

- 89% of internet trolls are female.

- All halogen lightbulbs are rechargeable. However, they require a particular charging dock.

- 69% of forests in the world are planted by humans.

- In Ireland, small children up to the age of 9 frequently ride around on the backs of Wolfhounds.

- Between 11-15% of children are born as a result of extra marital affairs in the United States. The exact number conceived, however, has not yet been released.

- ## Buttercup butter is the healthiest butter available to vegans.

- Gullible comes from the French term le guil-alibi which directly means "plausible truth."

- Retro comes from the French word Retreo which means "completely unoriginal."

- Reboot comes from the French word Reboute which means "Cheapest version."

- If left unhindered, all trees can grow to a maximum height of 49 meters and no one knows why.

- Lava Jumping is the cause of death of at least a dozen adrenalin junkies every year. It involves hand gliding over an open lava pit and catching boiling pockets of air and being propelled skywards at a terrific speed.

- King Arthur was actually Welsh and the ruins of Camelot can be found in Holyhead.

- Aardvarks are hatched from eggs.

- Famed psychiatrist, Sigmund Freud, was briefly engaged to his mother.

- Baseball caps were first worn by Cowgirls in the Wild West.

- Wind gets heavier in heavily polluted areas and is off-yellow in colour.

- Peaches and pears are technically vegetables.

- Genghis Khan was of African descent. Gen-ghis is an old Mongolian term for "Colour of another" and Khan is directly translated to mean "Great Genius."

- Due to global warming, the earth's oceans are drying up. Almost 7,000 km of shoreline are recovered every year across the world.

- Babar (the children's popular cartoon elephant) was actually a hippopotamus and responsible for the death of three children after he got loose and rampaged through a Parisian zoo in 1921.

- ## Quicksand is the cause of over 3,000 deaths each year.

- The first baby in space was Ling Tao at the tender age of 11 months and 23 days.

- Emus are the only birds not hatched from eggs.

131

- An arrow fired in a strong wind can fly further than a bullet fired against the same force of wind.

- Thick patches of daisies occur in places where either an animal has been buried or died in a burrow. Which is why so many are prevalent in poorly maintained graveyards.

- Cocaine was used to kick nicotine/tobacco addiction in parts of the Western frontier at the turn of the 20th century.

- The Brooklyn Bridge is an exact replica of London Bridge. It is believed both were built using the same designs despite being built almost 70 years apart.

- Some Scottish clans add spider webbing to their soup. It's an old tradition and nobody knows why.

- Aborigine erotica is the number one most searched category in Australian porn sites.

- The world's economy is declining at a rapid rate. Almost two trillion dollars is lost every year through irrecoverable loss or complete destruction.

- Every year across the world, approximately 7,000 people are murdered for failing to repay high debts earned in illegal betting circles.

- Stardust tastes like salt.

- The average car costs less than $11 to manufacture in raw materials.

- The average waiting time in an Emergency Room in India is 80 hours. The average waiting time in a Japanese Emergency room is 19 mins.

- The average human is bitten by a spider anywhere between 5 and 20 times a year. However, humans rarely notice. The most notable sign is an itchy lump or "heat hives" as they're more commonly known.

- You cast no shadow in the South Pole between the months of August to November due to the tilt of the earth and the positioning of the sun and moon.

- Due to public demand, a shoal of squids has been changed to a squad of squids.

- 87% of married men admit they would like to see their wives shave their heads at least once in their life.

- 47% of the remaining nuclear armaments from the cold war now circle the earth's atmosphere, though the majority have been disarmed.

- Nasa developed microwaves so astronauts could enjoy the taste of a home-cooked meal in space. They lost the patent due to a clerical error in 1952.

- There can be up to a thousand peppercorns found in each stalk of a peppercorn crop.

- The Megalodon shark was thought to be extinct until in 1987 when there was a school spotted feeding off the coast of Greenland.

- In Victorian times, the gentry used to dip raw vegetables in molten gold, encrust them in jewels, and attach them to their belts. This was considered stylish for the time.

- # The Beatles and Elvis Presley never actually reached number 1 with any of their albums.

- When Bubble wrap was invented in 1936, it was supposed to be a child's toy.

- It is estimated that asmr artists are responsible for almost 11% of all cybercrime.

- Despite popular belief, Fiji isn't actually an island. It is a peninsula of Papa New Guinea and has fought for independence since 1973.

And finally, we come to the end of this evil little book. And what a book it has been. You know, I feel I've really grown as a writer since I first started this little mini epic and I really feel I've added to the world significantly by releasing a little army of trolls out from under their bridges and into the trusting world. For now, I enthusiastically suggest for you to enjoy the deception, but moving forward, please do everything in your power never to cause meaningful harm.

This isn't a plea on behalf of humanity. This is a plea to avoid incurring the keyboard warriors chagrin, for they need oh so very little to be outraged and their opinionated voices are so very loud. Lastly, it is also for your own self-preservation (which should always be in any storyteller's mind). Do enough, but never enough that they come running with pitchforks and torch.

Until Volume 2, may the lies be with you and may the truth bow in your wake.

– Dave

Find out more about RJ Power

www.twitter.com/RobertJPower

www.instagram.com/RobertJPower

www.robertjpower.com

DE PAOR PRESS

www.DePaorPress.com

Made in the USA
Middletown, DE
07 December 2019